Artlist Coll
THE DOG

W9-CSL-904

Hollywood Spaniel

By Howie Dewin

SCHOLASTIC INC.

New York   Toronto   London   Auckland   Sydney

Mexico City   New Delhi   Hong Kong   Buenos Aires

For the Haggard Girls

ISBN-13: 978-0-545-10482-1
ISBN-10: 0-545-10482-3

© 2009 artlist INTERNATIONAL

Published by Scholastic Inc. All rights reserved.

12 11 10 9 8 7 6 5 4 3 2 1   9 10 11 12 13/0

Designed by Deena Fleming
Printed in the U.S.A.
First printing, January 2009

Kara is a Cocker Spaniel. Her first memory was of being lost in a strange neighborhood. Then a young girl lifted her up. That was the moment that nine-year-old Jessy found Kara and saved her life! Today, Jessy and her family have given Kara a loving home, even though they are poor. Kara has always wanted to help her human family. But she has never known how. . . .

Chapter 1

Kara the Cocker Spaniel looked out the window. She liked to know what was happening outside their Los Angeles apartment. It was a rough neighborhood. Kara wanted to be prepared. After all, she had a human girl named Jessy to take care of.

"Are you waiting for someone, Kara?"

Nine-year-old Jessy giggled at her dog. It was funny to see Kara studying the cars and people outside.

Kara's head popped up. Was it dinnertime?

Jessy wrapped her arms around Kara. Then she rested her elbows on the windowsill. Most of the cars parked along the street were old. There were trash cans on the street. Some lay on their side.

"It looks like the garbagemen have been

here," Jessy said to Kara. "They never put the cans back in the right place!"

They miss a lot of the trash too! thought Kara. The dog looked at the paper, glass, and plastic that littered the street.

"Jessy! Can I help feed Kara today?" Jessy's little sister, Jordan, asked. Jordan was only five years old. But she wanted to do everything Jessy did. "I want to learn how to feed her."

Kara jumped down from the windowsill.

"I'm starving!" Kara barked.

"Okay, okay!" Jessy said. "Don't bark, Kara! And Jordan, you can feed her." In the kitchen, Jessy opened the cabinet where Kara's food was kept. The shelf was bare.

Kara felt a rumble in her stomach. The empty cabinet made her feel twice as hungry.

"Mom?" Jessy called gently. "There's no food for Kara."

Jessy's mom came into the kitchen. She was still wearing her work clothes. They were covered in paint. Jessy's mom was a wonderful artist, but that wasn't how she earned money for the family. She painted people's apartments. It wasn't always easy to find work.

"I'm sorry, honey. I was a little short of money at the grocery store yesterday. I had to put back a few things."

Jessy nodded. She hated making her mother feel bad. Her father was the landlord of their building. That meant their rent was paid. But they depended on Mom to pay for groceries and other things.

"I'm getting a check tomorrow, and we'll stock up," said Mom. "We'll be fine!"

"I was going to feed Kara," Jordan said with a pout.

"If you stop whining, you can come with me to the animal shelter," Jessy told her sister. "I'm sure we can get some dog food there."

Jordan's face brightened.

Kara rushed to the hook by the door. She grabbed her leash. This was Kara's best trick.

"Thanks, honey," Jessy's mom said to her softly.

Kara brought the leash to Jessy. She loved

pleasing her girl. But this time, Jessy was looking at her mom. Kara wished that she could do something to make her family look less worried. She also wished for something to eat!

Kara stepped around a piece of broken glass as they left their building. Jessy and Jordan walked behind her on the way to the animal shelter. Kara kept a lookout for glass and anything else that could cut her paw.

BANG!

Jessy jumped. Jordan yelped. What made that noise?

"It's okay," Jessy said. "It was just a car backfiring."

Kara always hoped it was *just* a car noise. Sometimes scary things happened in their neighborhood.

Kara couldn't remember ever living anywhere else. But she knew she must have, because of the story Jessy often told her. Jessy loved telling how they had adopted Kara when she found her on the street.

Suddenly, a taxicab screeched past.
"Watch out!" Jessy's shout brought Kara

Some dogs are more comfortable living in a city apartment than others. There are several things to think about: the size of the dog, the need for exercise, basic behavior (for example, hounds are loud!), and whether the dog gets bored without a job to do. Here are a few breeds that tend to do well in apartments: Chihuahua, Dachshund, Pug, Basset Hound, Whippet, Old English Sheepdog!

out of her daydream. "Kara! You have to be more careful."

Kara wished she could help Jessy and her family.

"Hey, Kara!" A familiar dog's voice called out to the Cocker Spaniel. "It's nice to see you!"

Kara smiled. It was Jorge the Chihuahua.

"Oh, my beautiful Kara, how can you be so cruel?" Jorge said with a smile. Jorge pretended

Hey, Kara!

JORGE

his heart was breaking. Kara looked away so he wouldn't see her blush.

"Say hello to me! Say 'Hello, Jorge, the Friendly Neighborhood Chihuahua!'"

"Hi, Jorge! Good dog, Jorge!" Jordan and Jessy responded to the Chihuahua's barks.

"I think he has a crush on Kara." Jessy giggled to her sister.

Suddenly, Kara stopped in her tracks.

Straight ahead a crowd had gathered. Kara's heart pounded. What was this new danger?

One of the Cocker Spaniel's distinctive features is its long, hanging ears.

Chapter 2

Kara stepped in front of the girls. If there was trouble, Kara wanted to protect her family. Kara sniffed the air. Usually, she could smell danger. But she didn't smell it in this crowd.

"What's going on?" Jessy asked a tall neighbor who could see over everyone.

"Movie," the man mumbled. "Bunch of actors taking over and stopping traffic! *Humph!*" The man walked away.

"A movie!" Jessy whispered to Jordan.

"Wow!" Jordan whispered.

"Let's get closer," Jessy said quietly.

Kara tried to forget her hunger. She could see how much Jessy wanted to get a look at the movie set. They wiggled through the sea of legs.

"Pardon me," said Jessy.

Kara quietly slinked along behind them.

At last, Kara could see light ahead. They were just behind the front line of the crowd. Kara and her girls strained to see past the legs in front of them.

The Muffy Sinclair Show

Lilly

"Those must be the actors' legs." Jessy giggled. "I wonder who's in this movie!"

The girls carefully stood so they wouldn't block anyone. They inched up until they were in the front line.

It was a big movie set with hundreds of bright lights! Twenty people ran around setting things up. Jessy held tight to Jordan's hand.

Kara wedged herself between the two girls. She had to admit it was exciting.

"That's Muffy St. Clair," Jessy squealed. "She's the girl from the TV show with the dog that looks just like Kara!"

Kara pricked up her ears. Now she really forgot how hungry she was. Jessy rested her hand on Kara's head.

"Let's go, people! We need to get this shot!" A large man with a brimmed hat was pacing around the camera. Jessy decided he must be the director.

"Where's Lilly?" Jordan asked excitedly. "Where's her dog?"

"I don't see Lilly, but that's definitely Muffy

St. Clair!" Jessy squeaked.

"I saw the dog a while ago," said a boy nearby. "But now they're having trouble with that fire hydrant. Maybe they're on a break."

Jessy studied the young actress. Muffy was about the same age as Jessy. The actress was sitting in a tall chair under an umbrella. She was wearing sunglasses and a fur-trimmed sweater. There were lots of people all around her.

"I can't believe Muffy St. Clair is in our neighborhood!" Jessy whispered.

Kara couldn't believe it, either. She and Jessy watched *The Muffy St. Clair Show* every week. It was their favorite show. Muffy was always getting into trouble. But the best part was that her smart and brave Cocker Spaniel, Lilly, was always saving her!

"Somebody tell me what's going on!" the director shouted. "We're losing the light!"

Kara put her nose up. She could smell tension in the air.

Everyone is getting upset, thought Kara.

Then Kara caught sight of something: a golden furry ear behind a stack of crates. It looked just like her ear! Kara let out a little yip. She had just spotted the famous TV dog. She was looking at the ear of Lilly, the smart and brave Cocker Spaniel!

Kara let out another tiny yelp, but then stopped herself. She didn't want to make a scene.

Cocker Spaniels were bred to be hunting dogs. They got their name from the bird they were so good at hunting-woodcocks. But today they are popular house dogs and glamorous show dogs. They are easy to train. They like to work, and they like people. They are generally cheerful, playful, and get along with other animals.

"Do you wish you were a movie star, Kara?" Jessy asked her dog.

Kara was in awe at seeing her hero. But that wasn't the amazing thing. Lilly was staring back at *her*!

"Are they going to shoot soon?" Jessy asked the boy next to her.

"I don't know," the boy said. "I think they fixed the hydrant. I don't know what the problem is now."

"No!" A whiny screech sailed into the air.

Everyone in the crowd looked at Muffy St. Clair.

"I won't sit on that stoop until it's been scrubbed!" Muffy declared.

"Well," whispered the boy, "I guess that's what's wrong. She's a spoiled brat!"

Kara wasn't listening anymore. She was staring at Lilly. She bowed her head. She wanted Lilly to know how much she respected her.

When Kara lifted her head, she couldn't believe what she saw. Lilly was bowing back.

Then the famous dog tilted her head to the side.

Kara tilted her head back.

Lilly thrust her head again. Kara couldn't believe it. There was no question about it. Lilly was inviting Kara over. Lilly was saying she wanted to be friends!

Kara didn't think twice. She slipped away from Jessy and crawled around the edge of the crowd. Then she slipped behind the crates.

It seemed like a dream. She was standing right in front of Lilly. Lilly let out a little friendly huff. Then she touched her nose to Kara's nose!

The Cocker Spaniel is the smallest of the Sporting Group of dogs.

Chapter 3

Kara tried to find her voice but couldn't make a sound. Her tail wagged uncontrollably.

"Hi," Lilly said softly.

Kara stared shyly.

"What's your name?" asked Lilly.

"Umm," said Kara.

"Don't be nervous. I'm a Cocker Spaniel just like you."

Kara smiled. Lilly was really nice!

"Kara," she finally said. "My name is Kara. That's my girl over there. Her name is Jessy. We live right down the next block. We take walks here every day. There's a Chihuahua over there named Jorge. He likes me. I like you! We watch your show every week!"

Now Kara couldn't stop talking. She was so nervous!

Lilly laughed. "I guess you found your voice! It's nice to meet you. I never get to meet other Cocker Spaniels. I spend most of my time with Taz."

"Who's Taz?" Kara asked.

Lilly pointed her nose toward a man who was talking on a cell phone.

"He's my manager. He teaches me all the tricks I have to do."

Dogs have been in show business for hundreds of years. Before TV and movies, dogs performed with people on the stage. Dogs have also been longtime circus performers!

"That sounds like fun," Kara said.

"Sometimes," Lilly said softly.

"I bet you do lots of exciting things!" Kara said.

"I guess. But your life sounds pretty nice," Lilly said. Kara was surprised. Lilly's voice sounded sad.

"I have a really nice family," Kara agreed. "But—"

Before Kara could explain her family's troubles, the director interrupted.

"Okay! Are we ready, people? Get the dog! Let's shoot this scene!"

Suddenly, everyone was moving. People were grabbing things. Makeup was being touched up. Kara turned to run back to Jessy. But before she could move, a pair of hands picked her up.

She barked and looked to see who was carrying her.

"Come on, Lilly!" Taz, the dog manager, said to Kara.

"I'm Kara!" Kara barked.

"Oh, no!" hissed Taz. "Don't *you* cause a

problem now! We have enough problems with the brat kid!"

Kara struggled to break free. She turned to look for Jessy but couldn't believe her eyes. Lilly the TV dog was standing right next to Jessy. She had switched places with Kara! Jessy was petting Lilly! Jessy didn't realize it was the wrong dog!

Taz set Kara down next to the actress Muffy St. Clair. Kara was too frightened to move. The lights were blinding. She couldn't see anything. At last, her eyes adjusted. "Okay, Taz," the director growled. "It's time for the dog to earn her money!"

"Time for the hydrant trick," Taz whispered to Kara.

Taz opened his hand right under Kara's nose. The smell was delicious. Suddenly, Kara's hunger flooded back. She eagerly chomped the treat in Taz's hand.

"You're suddenly hungry!" Taz said. "That's good. Do the trick right the first time, and there are more where that came from!"

Taz made funny motions with his hands. Kara stared at him but didn't understand. She tilted her head.

"Jessy!" she barked.

"No barking!" the director said.

Taz looked at Kara sternly. He opened his hand. There were lots of treats sitting in his palm. Kara was so hungry!

"Open the hydrant, Lilly!" Taz hissed.

Not understanding, Kara tried to keep herself from drooling. She tried to figure out what she was supposed to do. She wanted Jessy. But she also wanted the food.

"Help!" she yelped.

Nobody understood her.

Chapter 4

"What's going on?" the director shouted. "Does the dog know the trick or not?"

"Give me a minute," Taz said.

He walked up to Kara and knelt down. He opened his hand and let her smell the treats. Kara's mouth watered. She tried to grab one. Taz closed his hand before she could get one.

"Hydrant!" Taz said in a quiet voice.

Kara could sense how upset he was getting. She tried to understand what he wanted. But her head kept turning toward Jessy. She kept trying to call for her girl.

"Clear the set!" the director shouted. "The dog is distracted. Get these people out of here!"

Kara whipped around. She saw the crowd being pushed back. Kara could no longer find Jessy in the crowd.

"No!" barked Kara. *"Jessy! Don't go!"*

"Quiet!" hissed Taz. His hand wrapped around her muzzle. He opened his hand with the treats again.

"Do the trick. Get the food," Taz whispered. "Set!"

Set? thought Kara. *What does "set" mean?*

"Okay," Taz said to the director. "We're ready. She's set."

Oh, thought Kara, set means ready. *Wait! What are we ready for?* Kara looked at the director. She looked at Taz. Her heart pounded.

"Quiet on the set!" someone shouted.

"And action!" called the director.

Taz made the funny hand signals again.

A small whimper escaped from Kara. She was so hungry. She just wanted the food in Taz's hand.

Just give me the food, she thought. *Then maybe I can understand what you want.*

Kara walked over to Taz. She tried sitting and asking nicely for the food. But the director threw down his hat.

"What have I done to deserve this?" he cried.

"I can't work with the dog!" cried another voice. Kara turned to see Muffy standing up. She stamped her feet and shook her fists. "This

Young children and dogs are not always a good mix. It's important to choose the right breed (and the right dog) when there's a young child in the family. Young children don't always understand that a dog needs to be treated with loving care just like people do. Cocker Spaniels are among the best dogs when paired with children.

stupid dog gets all the attention, and for what? She can't even do a simple trick! I'm the star here! Why doesn't anyone understand that?"

Except for Muffy, the set was silent. Muffy stomped right over to Kara.

"You are the dumbest dog ever! I could never get away with being as stupid as you are! One little trick! That's all you have to do!" Muffy screamed.

Kara lowered her head. She squeezed her eyes shut. She had never smelled anyone so angry.

"What is so hard about this? You walk over here," Muffy explained.

Kara watched Muffy walk to the hydrant.

"You step behind it," Muffy shouted as she stepped behind the hydrant.

Now Kara was watching carefully. Muffy was the meanest girl she had ever met. But at least she was showing what Kara was supposed to do!

"And you take your stupid paw and push

down on this red lever!"

Muffy threw her arms in the air. People started crowding around her, trying to calm her. Muffy turned back to Kara.

"I have to get my hair done before the big party tonight. If you make me late—well, just see if you have a job tomorrow!"

Kara now understood why Lilly had tricked her. Lilly would have done *anything* to get away from Muffy. Now Kara also understood why Lilly had sounded so sad. Being the smart dog of Muffy St. Clair was not as much fun as it seemed.

I might have done the same thing, thought Kara.

"Okay," the director said calmly. "Let's do this."

Taz stared at Kara. He smiled and opened his hand.

I have to do this trick, thought Kara. *I have to get some food. Then I can think clearly and figure out how to escape.*

Kara went back to the spot where Taz had

placed her. She sat down.

"Set," said Taz.

Set, thought Kara. *Walk to the hydrant. Step behind it. Pull the lever. I can do this.*

"And . . ." said the director. "Action!"

Lady and the Tramp was a famous movie starring a Cocker Spaniel.

Chapter 5

"Hi, Mom!" called Jessy. "We're home. And we got some food for Kara!"

Lilly stepped slowly into the apartment. She had never seen anything like it. And she had never had to climb so many stairs! She always rode on elevators.

Stay calm, she told herself. *Act natural.*

"Hi, girls," Mom said. She met them at the door. "That was very smart of you, Jessy. Kara's lucky to have you."

Lilly was sniffing the floor.

"Did you hear that, Kara? Mom says you're lucky to have me!"

Lilly didn't look up. *What are all these new smells?* wondered Lilly.

"Kara!" Jessy said. "What's wrong? What do you smell?"

Lilly realized Jessy was talking to her. She gave a little yip and rushed to Jessy.

"You must be really hungry. Huh, girl?" Jessy said.

"I still get to help!" Jordan piped up.

A minute later, Jordan put a plate in front of Lilly.

Lilly put her nose to the plate.

Whoa! This is food? she thought. *No way!*

"Are you sick?" Jessy asked. She studied her dog's face. "Something isn't right with Kara," Jessy said.

"Maybe she's tired," Mom said. "Don't worry. I'm sure she's fine."

"No, really, " Jessy said. "It's weird."

Lilly nuzzled Jessy. She had to make the girl believe she was Kara. Even if the food was awful and everything smelled musty, it was better than being with Muffy!

★ ★ ★ ★ ★ ★

Meanwhile, the real Kara was in the back-seat of a big black car. The car pulled up to a huge white building.

"Well, here we are, Lilly," said Taz. "Home, sweet home."

Home? thought Kara. She stared at great big pillars. *I wonder which floor our apartment is on.*

"It wasn't your best day, little dog," said Taz. "Try to shake it off. We have to get ready for tonight!"

Kara shuddered. She had finally gotten the trick right, but it took a long time. It was awful to smell so much anger in the air.

"Tonight is the premiere of *Dog Day Delight*," said Taz.

Premiere? Kara stared at Taz. *What's a premiere?*

Kara could smell that Taz was excited.

"I think this is going to be one of your best movies," he said. "It's always exciting to see them for the first time, don't you think?"

Taz opened the mansion's front doors. Kara froze. There were no apartments. It was just one big house! Kara shook her head. Maybe she was seeing things.

"Lilly?" Taz said.

Kara looked at him. She felt dizzy.

"Step through the door, please. I'd like to close it." Taz laughed. "You're really off today, aren't you?"

"Welcome home! Welcome home!" Kara turned to see two people rushing toward her.

"Hi, Felice," Taz said to the woman with an apron. "How are you, Buzz?" he said to the man in a white jacket.

"How's our star?" asked Felice. "Ready for a nibble?"

She lifted Kara up. Felice carried her off. Kara began to smell wonderful things.

What is that amazing smell? she thought.

"I'll need her in twenty minutes!" Buzz said. "She needs a full brush before we leave for the premiere."

They entered a kitchen. It was huge, shiny, and filled with food. Kara's eyes grew wider. Felice placed Kara gently on a fluffy pillow. The pillow was atop a stool pulled up to a counter.

I eat at the table? thought Kara. It was

unbelievable. *This is great!*

"There you are, my love," said Felice. Kara liked Felice already. "And here is a little kidney pie to start. Your steak is almost ready!" Felice put a silver dish in front of her. Kara's entire face went into the dish. She didn't even stop to breathe.

Teaching dogs tricks takes lots of patience. Some breeds learn faster and easier than others. But any dog needs time to learn tricks. It's best to work a little bit every day instead of a long time all at once. Training sessions should feel like play for your dog. If your dog is having fun, he will learn tricks easier. And don't forget the reward treats!

"Wow!" Felice laughed. "I guess you worked hard today!"

"It was a tough day," said Taz as he walked into the room. "She seemed confused. She didn't remember the tricks we'd worked on."

"Everybody has bad days," said Felice.

"Well, we have a lot to do in the next few days. There's a photo shoot tomorrow for *Dog People,* and then we have to be back on the set. Next week, she starts that new feature film!"

Kara finally looked up from her dish. She had never had such a fine meal.

Just tell me the trick and I'll do it! thought Kara. *Because this is the life!*

Buzz arrived and carried Kara to another room. Now she was being brushed and combed. It felt so good.

"Well, you seem happy!" Buzz smiled. "Let's work on those ears!"

By the time the big black car pulled up, Kara felt like a new dog. She saw her reflection in a mirror. She never knew her ears could be so fluffy!

Buzz carried her to the car. He put her on a velvet pillow in the backseat.

Oh, yeah! she thought. *I like pillows, and I like this soft stuff, and I like being a star!*

I like being a star!

★ ★ ★ ★ ★ ★

"Let's go for a walk, Kara," Jessy said.

Lilly could tell the girl was worried. Lilly knew she had to do her best acting if she didn't want to get sent back to Muffy.

"Get your leash!" Jessy said.

Leash! Lilly knew that word. *She wants the leash!*

Lilly looked quickly around the room. She spotted the leash on the hook by the door. She ran to it and lifted it off the hook.

Jessy took the leash with a smile.

That was close, thought Lilly.

"Let's go," Jessy said. They headed outside.

Lilly had to work hard to stay focused.

Don't sniff everything! she told herself.

Lilly had to be careful not to step on the sharp things on the sidewalk.

"Oh, my *beautiful* Kara!" Lilly heard a funny voice. She turned toward it. There was a little dog sitting in a window.

Lilly remembered something Kara had told her: *"There's a Chihuahua over there named Jorge.*

He likes me."

Lilly turned to say hello to Jorge. She was so glad she could use his name. He would never know she wasn't Kara. But Jorge started to growl.

"You are not my beautiful Kara!" the dog snapped. "Who are you? What have you done with my Kara?"

Jorge barked. Jessy stared in disbelief. She had never see Jorge act like this. Jorge loved Kara! Why was he growling and snapping?

Jessy looked at her dog.

Now she was certain.

Something was definitely wrong!

What have you done with my Kara?

Chapter 6

The first light of morning came through the window. Kara had barely slept.

It had been such an exciting night. She walked on a bright red rug into the fancy building. Lights flashed. Everybody called her name. The treats never stopped.

Maybe I'm dreaming, thought Kara. She laid her head on her soft pillow. She had her own room!

This is the nicest room I've ever seen, she thought. *It's so much bigger and brighter than Jessy's—*

Suddenly, Kara's head popped up. She felt like she had just awoken from a dream. She had forgotten Jessy for a whole day! A pit filled her stomach. How could she have forgotten about Jessy? She loved Jessy, and Jessy loved her. How could she have walked away?

The smell of steak suddenly floated into her bedroom. Felice was cooking breakfast already!

Breakfast! Kara jumped down off the bed.

Welcome to another day of glorious food! she thought. *I will just eat breakfast, and then figure out how to find Jessy.*

"Good morning, Lilly!" Taz said as Kara trotted into the hallway. "Big photo shoot today!"

Kara thought about how good it felt when Buzz brushed her fur.

A whole day of brushing! she thought.

She wagged her tail and gave a little yip to Taz. Then she headed to the kitchen.

★ ★ ★ ★ ★ ★

Later that day, Jessy hurried home after school. She was anxious to see Kara. Maybe she would seem more like herself today. She burst through the front door.

"Let's go for a walk, Kara!" Jessy said.

Lilly jumped up. She ran for the leash.

"That's a good girl!" Jessy smiled.

Lilly was relieved. There was less doubt on the girl's face. That was good, because Lilly didn't want to get caught. She enjoyed lying around. Lilly never got to do that in her old life. There was always somewhere to be. Someone was always telling her what to do.

I can get used to the food, Lilly told herself. *And I can definitely get used to relaxing!*

"Jessy," Jessy's mom called to her. "I need some milk. Could you and Kara stop at the deli?"

"Sure, Mom!" Jessy smiled. "Let's go, Kara!"

Lilly wagged her tail. They headed down to the street.

★ ★ ★ ★ ★ ★

"This way, Lilly!" called the man behind the camera. "Over here! Now here!"

Kara could barely keep up. She was getting better at figuring out what Taz wanted her to

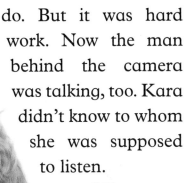

do. But it was hard work. Now the man behind the camera was talking, too. Kara didn't know to whom she was supposed to listen.

"She seems a little confused today," said the man behind the camera.

"She's okay," Taz said. But he gave Kara a worried look.

Kara knew she was about to get in trouble again. She concentrated on Taz's face and hands. Suddenly, she understood he wanted her to walk back and forth while looking at the camera.

"There you go!" said Taz. "That's it!"

Kara's heart sailed! She couldn't help it. She really wanted to make Taz happy. She wanted the treats and the soft bed. She wanted Felice and Buzz to like her. She wanted to be the best Hollywood dog she could be.

"I think we've got it!" the man behind the camera said. "Nice work!"

Nice work! Kara said to herself. *I did nice work!*

The next thing she knew, Taz gave her a handful of treats!

"Okay!" said Taz. "Now all we have to do is get back on track with Muffy St. Clair!"

Kara froze. She had put Muffy out of her mind. Now she remembered the most spoiled girl in the whole world. She remembered how Muffy blamed everything on the dog! Kara looked up at Taz.

"Don't worry, girl." He smiled. "That's not until tomorrow!"

★ ★ ★ ★ ★ ★

Jessy stood in line at the deli. She had to pay for the milk before she and Kara walked home. Kara was tied up outside. She stared at her dog through the deli door. As she waited, her eyes drifted across the newspaper headlines on the counter. One photo jumped out at her.

The headline read: "Hollywood Pays a Visit—Glamorous Week for Our Neighborhood!" There was a picture of Muffy St. Clair and her dog, Lilly. Jessy was amazed again at how much Lilly looked like Kara. She stared out the door at Kara again.

They look more alike than ever, Jessy thought, her stomach feeling funny.

"Next!" called the man behind the counter. Jessy put the paper back on the counter. She paid for the milk.

"Let's go home by Jorge's house," Jessy said. "He was so upset yesterday. We should see if he's okay."

Lilly tried not to pull back on the leash. But everything in her wanted to go the other way.

Jorge knows, Lilly thought. *He's going to ruin everything!*

But there was no choice. If she refused to walk, Jessy would know there was a problem.

So Lilly kept her eyes down and tried to hurry past the Chihuahua's block.

"There it is again!" Jorge shouted as soon as he saw Lilly. "There is the imposter! You are not Kara!"

Imposter!

Dogs have good senses. Sometimes it seems like they know things that humans couldn't know. Some scientists say that dogs have an electromagnetic sense. That sense allows them to feel earth tremors and vibrations that humans don't feel. This might be why it seems like they can "predict" earthquakes and other natural disasters. Whether that is true or not, we know that dogs are excellent hunters. That means they are good at telling who is a friend and who is a foe.

"What's wrong, Jorge?" Jessy asked.

"Bring my Kara back! You go!" Jorge barked.

Lilly's temper flared.

"Leave me alone!" Lilly barked back. *"It's not your business!"*

"Kara!" Jessy shouted. "Stop that!"

Jessy pulled back on her dog's leash. Lilly felt the tug, and it made her madder. She couldn't believe a Chihuahua was going to ruin her plan. She would have to go back to that terrible little actress.

Jessy pulled again on Kara's leash. Without meaning to, Lilly turned her head. *"STOP IT!"* Lilly growled at Jessy. Jessy froze. Kara had never ever snapped at her.

Lilly realized she had made a terrible mistake. She lowered her head. She tried to tell Jessy she was sorry. But it was too late.

"You're not Kara," Jessy whispered.

The Cocker Spaniel breed originated in Europe.

Chapter 7

"**W**ait!" shouted Lilly. She ran behind Jessy. "*I can explain. Please stop running!*"

Jessy held the leash as she ran all the way home. She had to tell her mom. Mom would help fix this. Where was the *real* Kara? How did this happen?

When Jessy got home, she turned to Lilly. It seemed strange to bring her indoors now. She wasn't Kara. Jessy knew it for sure. Now it felt like she was bringing a strange dog into the house.

Lilly felt awful. She didn't want to get sent back. But she felt bad for tricking Jessy and Kara, too. Even her ears hung low.

"I shouldn't bring you inside," Jessy said. "I don't even know who you are. . . ."

Lilly lowered herself so that her belly touched

the ground. She put her head on her paws.

"Oh, come on. I'm not going to abandon you in the street." Jessy sighed.

She hurried up the stairs.

"Mom!" she shouted. "Mom!"

"What?" her mother shouted. "I'm on the phone with work."

Jessy ran to the kitchen. She stood in front of her mother. She put her hands on her hips. She tried to make it clear that she had to talk *now*!

Finally, her mother hung up.

"What is so important?" her mother asked. She sounded annoyed. But Jessy didn't care. This was more important than staying out of trouble.

"This isn't Kara! I don't know who it is, but it's not our dog!"

Her mother stared at her. "What are you talking about?" Mom finally said.

"That's why she hasn't eaten, and didn't know about the leash, and keeps smelling everything. It's not Kara!"

Jessy's mom turned away.

"Of course it's Kara. Now stop bothering me, Jessy. I'm trying to line up some work. It's important that I make these calls."

Lilly pulled gently on the leash. She tried to lead Jessy away from the conversation.

Jessy felt Lilly's tug and tugged back.

"Mom! I'm telling you the truth. We have a strange dog in the house, and I don't know where Kara is!"

"And how do you think this amazing switch happened?"

Jessy was about to blurt out, "I don't know!" But she stopped. It was like being hit by lightning. She suddenly realized what had happened.

"I'll tell you," Jessy said slowly. She looked down at Lilly. Then she looked back at her mother. "I know exactly what happened—and I know who this dog is!"

★ ★ ★ ★ ★ ★

"Okay!" shouted a movie assistant. "Quiet on the set!"

"Let's get off to a better start than yesterday,"

the director said to Kara.

"Do you really think that stupid mutt understands you?" asked Muffy. "That dog doesn't understand even *Woof*!"

"And action!" the director snapped.

Kara concentrated. She was pretty sure she understood the moves. She was supposed to go to Muffy. Then pick up a mug in her teeth. Go down the stairs. Go to the fire hydrant. Turn the lever and fill the mug with water. Then she was supposed to bring the mug back to Muffy.

It was going perfectly. She had the mug. She was down the stairs. But then the lever was . . . stuck!

"Cut!" cried the director.

"It isn't the dog's fault," Taz said. "The lever is stuck."

"Fix the lever!" The director threw his arms up in the air.

Kara looked at Taz. Did he really understand it wasn't her fault?

I'm getting tired of acting with a fire hydrant, thought Kara.

* * * * * *

"Okay, so who is this mystery dog standing in my kitchen?" Jessy's mom asked.

"Yeah," Jordan piped up, "who is it?"

Mom had her hands on her hips. Jessy knew she was about to get mad. She had to make her understand.

"It's Muffy St. Clair's dog, Lilly!" Jessy exclaimed. "They got switched when we visited that movie set the other day!"

Jordan squealed with delight. She fell to her knees and crawled over to Lilly.

"Lilly!" Jordan screeched.

"A big Hollywood star?" her mom said sarcastically. "I have a big Hollywood star in my house?"

"It's true! I swear!" Jessy pleaded.

"Jessy." Her mother's voice was stern. "I don't have time for this."

Jessy walked out of the kitchen. What could she do now? She stared at Lilly. Lilly wagged her tail.

"I'm sorry, Lilly," Jessy said. "I'm sure you're a nice dog. But I miss Kara."

Lilly hung her head. It was hopeless. She was going to be sent back.

Jessy knew what she had to do. She grabbed the movie-star dog and ran out the door. They had to get onto that set. Jessy had to convince everyone that her dog had been switched!

★ ★ ★ ★ ★ ★

"I can't stand it!" screamed Muffy. "I can't stand another whole day of smelling wet dog!"

The child star stood up. She stamped her feet. Nobody looked her in the eye.

"All day! Every day! All I smell is wet dog! I want that dog kept on the other side of the set. I will not have my trailer near her!"

Nobody moved.

"Do I make myself clear?"

Suddenly, people started moving. Taz lifted Kara and whisked her away from Muffy.

But I'm not even wet, thought Kara. *That is the meanest girl I've ever met! Imagine if she ever met Jessy—*

Dogs get sad just like people do. When a dog is sad, he will sleep more or have less energy, just like some sad people. He will be less interested in playing games. He might not want to go for a walk. Dogs pick up on human emotions, too. So if you're sad, your dog might be, too. Some quick, energetic games often help everybody feel better.

The pit in Kara's stomach returned. Jessy. Kara missed Jessy so much. Jessy was the finest girl in the world. She would never say all those horrible things. In that moment, all Kara wanted was to see Jessy again.

Kara let out a whimper.

I miss Jessy.

"Don't let her get to you," Taz whispered. "She's just a brat!"

Jessy. Kara whimpered. But Taz didn't understand.

★ ★ ★ ★ ★ ★

"I'm sorry, miss," said the movie guard. "But your name has to be on this list." He pointed to his clipboard. "Nobody else is allowed in."

Jessy could feel tears welling up. She was so close. She could see the movie set. Her dog was so close, but Jessy couldn't get to her.

"Please!" Jessy begged the guard. "You have to understand, sir. I just want my dog back."

"I can't help you," he said.

"But my dog got switched with Muffy St. Clair's dog!"

The guard laughed. "That's a good one," he said. "I haven't heard that one before. Okay. Tell me your story."

Jessy told him what had happened. By the end of her story, the guard had stopped laughing.

"Okay," said the guard. "It seems unlikely. But I'm going to let you through."

"Thank you! Oh, thank you!" she shouted.

Jessy stepped quickly through the gate and pulled on Lilly's leash. But the leash flew through the air. An empty collar landed at her feet.

Jessy spun around. She looked at the spot where the dog had been.

The movie-star dog was gone.

Chapter 8

I'll *just keep running*, Lilly said to herself. *If I can't stay with Jessy, then I'll find a new home.*

The little Cocker Spaniel wanted to run away. But she was too scared. How would she feed herself? How would she keep herself from being hurt by bigger dogs? She wasn't prepared for real life.

She ran until she found herself on a familiar block.

"Oh, see it run! There goes the faker!"

Jorge was sitting in his window. He was barking angrily at Lilly. Lilly didn't have enough spirit to yell back. She just sat down in front of Jorge's window. She stared at the Chihuahua.

"What is this? The faker is going to stare at Jorge?"

"I just want a normal life," Lilly said in a small voice. "I want to live with a family and be a regular dog."

Jorge stared at Lilly. He was puzzled. "What is this? Little faker dog is not from a happy home?"

Where is my Kara?

"It's a nice home . . . it's just not a family. Not really. Everybody in my life works for me."

Jorge laughed so hard he almost fell out

of the window. "Oooh! You are a funny dog! Everybody works for you! That is *fu-u-u-u-nny!*"

"It's true," Lilly said. "I'm the Muffy St. Clair dog. Don't you recognize me?"

Jorge's eyes grew large. Slowly, his little head started to bob.

"Yes! Yes! I see it now. You are the movie-star pup. How did this happen? Where is my Kara?"

Now Jorge looked concerned.

"Don't worry. Jessy has gone to get her. She'll be back in no time, and I'll be gone."

"Ooh," said Jorge, "little movie-star dog. I'm sorry you're so sad."

Suddenly, a pair of hands grabbed Lilly.

"That was not nice," Jessy said to her. "You shouldn't have run away!"

★ ★ ★ ★ ★ ★

"I NEED MY SUNGLASSES! THE DOG ATE MY SUNGLASSES! WOULD SOMEONE AROUND HERE DO SOMETHING?"

Muffy was screaming. Kara had to put her

Many dogs have become famous movie stars. The most famous of all might be Pal. Pal was the beautiful collie who was the original Lassie. Pal got his big break in 1943 when he was hired as a stand-in but ended up stealing the show! Many of Pal's children, grandchildren, and great-grandchildren have continued to play Lassie since then.

paws over her ears.

She is worse than ever, thought Kara. *I don't want to be a movie-star dog anymore.*

All the treats and attention didn't matter. Kara's heart had been growing heavier all day. The only thing she could think of was Jessy. She was sorry. She had been a bad friend. She had let the bright lights and fancy food make her forget who she was. She had forgotten the most important person in her life.

If I can just see Jessy, thought Kara, *I promise I will never again forget what is important!*

"NOT THESE SUNGLASSES! I NEED MY POLKA-DOT SUNGLASSES!" Muffy was throwing things now.

Kara let out a whimper.

"Come on, Lilly," Taz said. "It's time to work."

Kara's heart sank. She was tired of working so hard. She didn't want to figure out any more of Taz's hand signals. She never wanted to see a hydrant again. But mostly, she wanted to be with the people who loved her.

★ ★ ★ ★ ★ ★

"This will have to do," Jessy said. She held up some

thick twine. "We are going back to that movie set, Miss Movie Star Dog. We need to straighten this out!"

Lilly looked at her. She wished Jessy knew she was sorry for the trick she played. She wished Jessy could love her as much as Jessy seemed to love Kara.

Jessy tied the twine to an old beat-up collar she had found at home. She put it around Lilly's neck.

"Let's go," she said.

They ran all the way back to the movie set. The same guard was still on duty.

"Ah! The old 'switcheroo' dog is back!" the guard said with a laugh.

"You said I could go in," Jessy said.

"Yes, I did," he said. He opened the gate wide enough for them to slip through. Lilly wanted to pull away, but she didn't. She had promised herself that this time she would do the right thing. Nobody was facing them except Muffy. At first, Muffy was the only one who saw them. Lilly shuddered at the sight of her.

"I CAN'T STAND IT!" screamed Muffy. "IT'S A NIGHTMARE! ONE DUMB DOG IS NOT ENOUGH? NOW WE HAVE TO HAVE TWO?"

Lilly closed her eyes and tried to disappear. A dozen people turned to see what Muffy was screaming about now. Several people gasped. Taz looked at Lilly. Then he looked at the dog he had *thought* was Lilly. The director put his head in his hands.

"Who are you, and why have you brought another horrible dog to my set?" Muffy snapped at Jessy.

Jessy was shocked. How could Muffy St. Clair be so mean?

"This is your dog," Jessy said bravely. Then she pointed to Kara. "And that's mine."

Chapter 9

"*Jessy! Jessy!*" Kara barked her name again and again. She ran and jumped into her girl's arms.

Taz and the crew stared in disbelief. Tears ran down Jessy's face. Kara licked the tears away.

"Well, I guess there's no doubt whose dog is whose!" Taz finally said. He walked over to the real Lilly. "So where have *you* been?" he asked.

Jessy lowered Kara to the ground and turned to Taz. "She's been living with me," she said. Then Jessy told everyone what she had figured out.

"I knew something was funny!" said Taz. He smiled at Kara. "But I have to tell you, your dog did very well acting like Lilly. I can't believe how well she did!"

A lost dog is a terrible thing for everyone involved. There are some things we can do to keep it from happening. Always be sure your dog has a collar and an identification tag. Vets can implant a microchip that helps to identify your dog if its collar comes off. Always keep your dog on a leash when out walking. Make sure fenced-in areas are secure. If your dog does get lost, spread the word as quickly as you can. Put up posters. Be sure to include a photograph of your dog. Include information about when and where your dog went missing.

LOST DOG

REWARD!

"Kara is the smartest dog ever!" Jessy beamed.

"And how did you do as a family dog?" Taz asked Lilly. But Lilly wasn't listening. Her eyes were closed. She felt like her heart was breaking.

"IF WE HAVE TO STOP ONE MORE TIME BECAUSE OF DOGS—"

Muffy sat down on a pillow on the stoop. She was in place to shoot the scene, but nobody was paying any attention to her.

"Are we going to shoot this stupid hydrant scene or not?"

Taz kneeled down in front of Lilly. "Not too happy to be back?"

Lilly raised her head and looked into her trainer's eyes.

"I'm sorry she's such a brat," Taz whispered. He scratched behind Lilly's ears. Lilly realized she had missed Taz.

"ALL ANYONE CARES ABOUT HERE ARE DOGS! WHAT ABOUT *ME*?"

Lilly glared at Muffy. Then she looked at Kara. Kara was glaring at Muffy, too. Lilly huffed a little. Kara turned to her. The two dogs locked eyes. Without another sound, they both turned to Muffy. They walked together to the hydrant. The two dogs each put a paw on the lever. Together, they pulled down. The hydrant opened wide. A huge flood came gushing out. It shot right at Muffy St. Clair!

There was a moment of silence. All anyone could hear was the gushing water. Even Muffy was too shocked to scream. But then she did. She screamed loudly!

"AAAUUGH! STOP! STOP THE WATER!"

The girl was soaked. A big pool formed around her.

"GONE! BOTH OF THEM! I WANT BOTH OF THEM GONE! TO THE POUND! THEY WILL NEVER WORK IN THIS TOWN AGAIN!"

But it was hard to hear her over the laughter. Not a single person was able to keep a straight face. Kara and Lilly both jumped up on their hind legs. They pressed their front paws together.

"I SAID STO-O-O-O-OP!"

"No!" came another voice. It was not a

familiar voice. "*You* stop! Stop right this minute, young lady."

Everyone on the set went quiet.

A woman who looked like Muffy walked up to the star.

"What do you think—" Muffy began to snap at the woman.

"I said quiet!" the woman said.

Muffy looked surprised.

"I am your mother, and I am telling you to be quiet. We have all had more than enough of your behavior. One more tantrum and I will break every contract. That will be the end of your stardom! Do you understand?"

Lilly and Kara sat quietly and waited for Muffy's answer. Lilly had never felt so happy. She couldn't believe Muffy was finally being told to behave!

"I'm waiting for an answer," said Muffy's mother.

Muffy meekly nodded.

Lilly and Kara barked in celebration.

"May I borrow your phone?" Jessy asked

Taz. "I want to call my parents and tell them where I am."

The crew started working again. Muffy tried to compose herself. The hair, costume, and makeup people worked to dry her off.

Jessy and Kara stood with Lilly and watched all the activity.

"Okay, people, can we *please* get back to work?" asked the director.

"We should go now," Jessy said to Taz.

"Thank you for taking such good care of Lilly," Taz said.

"Thanks for taking care of Kara," Jessy smiled.

Many of the crew members waved and said good-bye.

"Let's go home, Kara," Jessy whispered.

Kara turned to go. But suddenly she stopped.

Jessy stumbled as the leash pulled her back.

"What, Kara?" Jessy said.

Kara looked at Jessy. Then she turned back and walked toward the set.

"You want to stay here?" Jessy asked in disbelief. She could feel her throat tightening. "You don't want to come home?"

Chapter 10

Kara looked at Taz. She finally knew how she could help her family. She knew how they could have enough money. Maybe they could even move to a safer neighborhood!

"Train me!" Kara barked to Taz. "Then I can work, too!"

Taz seemed to understand Kara's barks.

"You know," said Taz, "I was thinking the same thing."

"What are you talking about?" Jessy asked.

"I think your dog wants a job!" Taz smiled. "And I would really like to give her one, if it's okay with you."

"A job?" Jessy said.

"Jessy!"

Jessy turned to see her mom rushing toward her.

"What's going on?" her mom asked when she reached her daughter.

"I give up!" the director said. "We're never going to get this movie shot!"

"I was right, Mom!" Jessy said. "Kara and the movie-star dog were switched. But now Kara wants to be a movie-star dog, too!"

Jessy told her mother everything that had happened.

"So you're saying our dog could be an *actor*?" Jessy's mom asked Taz.

"She's a smart dog, and Lilly has too much work. I'd be happy to be her trainer if you're interested."

Kara looked at Jessy and barked happily.

"Could she still live with us?" Jessy asked.

"Absolutely," said Taz. "I would take her only on workdays."

"Paid?" Jessy's mom said in disbelief.

Taz smiled. "Lilly makes a good living!"

"Excuse me," someone said in a small voice. "Excuse me, but I think we have a problem here."

Everyone turned toward Muffy. All around her was a puddle of paint. "I think the water from the hydrant made the paint run off the set," she said in a quiet and polite voice.

"Where's the art department?" cried the director. "We need a re-paint!"

"The painter is out sick," someone answered.

"My mom is a painter," Jessy called out.

The crew looked at Jessy's mom. Then all eyes turned back to the director.

"Fine! Someone do the paperwork. Get her hired!" the director ordered. "We need this set ready to go NOW!"

"I guess your whole family is going into show business," Taz said with a laugh.

Jessy laughed, too. Kara leaped up into Jessy's arms.

"Come with me," someone said to her mother. "We have to fill out a few forms, and then we'll put you to work!"

Lilly walked over to Jessy. She sat down and let out a soft bark.

"Do you forgive me?" Lilly asked.

Jessy knelt down and pulled both dogs toward her.

"This is amazing!" Jessy giggled.

Lilly rested her head on Jessy's lap.

I think I have a family, Lilly thought happily.

"Everything has worked out perfectly, Kara!" Jessy said.

Kara barked, and Jessy knew just what she meant.

"Just like in the movies!"